Saxon Tales

The King Who Threw Away His Throne

Bloomsbury Education
An imprint of Bloomsbury Publishing Plc

50 Bedford Square
London
WC1B 3DP
UK

1385 Broadway
New York
NY 10018
USA

www.bloomsbury.com

ISBN
PB: 978 1 4729 2920 4
ePub: 978 1 4729 2921 1
ePDF: 978 1 4729 2922 8

2 4 6 8 10 9 7 5 3 1

Typeset by Amy Cooper Design
Printed and Bound by CPI Group (UK) Ltd, Croydon CR0 4YY

TERRY DEARY

Saxon Tales

The King Who Threw Away His Throne

Illustrated by

Tambe

BLOOMSBURY EDUCATION
AN IMPRINT OF BLOOMSBURY

LONDON OXFORD NEW YORK NEW DELHI SYDNEY

Contents

1

The Fool

King Vortigern was a fool. Yes, I know. Kings are supposed to be wise. Old kings like Vortigern are supposed to be wiser than an owl, finer than a peacock and cleverer than a jackdaw. Vortigern was none of those things but, as I say, Vortigern was a fool. He had more brains in his long white beard than he did in his skull.

How do I know? I know because I was there. I was a servant in the royal court and it was a dangerous place to be.

How did a fool come to be king, you ask?

They say that when Vortigern was young – long before I was born – this Britain was ruled by the mighty Romans. They put Vortigern on the throne in South Britain. He was weak and the Romans knew he would do what they told him to do.

Then the Romans left and we Britons were as helpless as piglets in a pen. Our enemies gathered their strength.

When I first arrived at Vortigern's palace as a kitchen boy it had been calm. Then a messenger arrived on a sweating horse with fear in his face. 'Where is King Vortigern,' the man groaned.

'What's wrong?' the chief cook asked.

'Give me a cup of your best ale and I'll tell you,' the panting rider gasped.

The chief cook turned to me. 'Get the poor man a cup of ale, Mervyn.' As I walked past him to the palace pantry he whispered, 'The cheap stuff will be good enough for him.'

I hurried back with the cup. The rider pulled a face as he supped the bitter beer. 'If that's your best beer then I'd hate to taste your worst.'

The cook just said, 'Here's the captain of the guard. Give him your message.'

The rider rose to his feet. 'I've ridden all the way from York. I have a message for King Vortigern.'

The captain said, 'Take off your sword-belt and dagger and I'll let you see him.'

The messenger shrugged and dropped the belt to the floor of the hallway and followed the captain into the great hall. I picked up the half-empty cup of ale and followed.

Vortigern was playing chess with his son, Faustus. He was the youngest son with a nose like a ferret's snout and teeth to match. The king was stroking his beard as if he thought it would help his next move. He looked up with watery, hazel eyes and blinked. 'Greetings, my friend. I can see by the dust on your leggings that you've ridden a long way today.'

'Yes, my Lord. Three days ago I was in York.'

'Ah, York! the city of mellow stone and fine churches. How are the churches?'

'Burning, sire. Wild men from Scotland have been raiding further and further south. Three days ago they reached York.

They've killed King Constans, Lord of North Britain.'

Vortigern's thick eyebrows rose. 'Ah, such a shame. Poor Constans. I suppose that makes me the king of the whole of Britain now. All those northern taxes to fill my money chests.'

The messenger shook his head and road dust drifted down. 'There won't be much tax to collect,' he sighed. 'The Scots steal what they can move and burn what they can't. The peasants are starving.

Vortigern's blinking was faster. 'Oh dear. Why do these Scots have to be so unpleasant? We are neighbours. Why can't they stay on their side of Hadrian's Wall and live in peace with us?'

Now, I could have told him the answer to that. Farming is hard work. It killed my father and mother, which is why I ended up a kitchen servant. Farmers have to go

out to freeze in the winter snows and be baked in the summer sun, gathering the hay and shearing the sheep, hauling the animal food to the barns they have to build to keep out the wolves. Not many peasant men live past thirty years.

Why did the Scots raid the farms of North Britain? Because it was easier than farming.

Before anyone could explain this simple thing to this simple king, the great hall doors crashed open and a messenger even dustier than the one from York limped in. I handed him the ale cup because he looked like he needed something.

He took a mouthful. Then he spat it on the rushes on the floor. 'Dreadful news, King Vortigern. Britain is being invaded.'

The king gave his smile, as wise as an infant. 'I know my son. The Scots have reached York...'

'No, sire,' the messenger cut in. 'It's not the Scots. It's someone much worse. And they are in Kent to the east. Much closer than York. It's the Saxon hordes and they will be here within five days. We have to flee.'

2

The Bully

'Oh dear,' King Vortigern moaned. 'Oh dear, oh dear. Oh dear, oh dear, oh dear. Those Saxons are so very rough. Even worse than the Scots. We're doomed, Faustus,' he said to his son. 'We're doomed!'

Faustus snorted, 'No we're not, Pa.'

'Yes we are,' the captain of the guard said.

'Yes we are,' I muttered.

'Shut. Up,' Faustus said. He pulled me by the arm and stood me at the king's right hand. Then he pushed the Captain to the left of Vortigern. He pointed at me. 'You are the Scots.'

'No I'm not,' I argued.

'Shut. Up.' Faustus repeated. 'Now, Captain, you are the Saxons. And here in the middle,' he said, pointing at his father, 'we have King Vortigern. You can't both attack him and steal his treasures.'

'My treasures? No one's getting my treasures,' Vortigern said and shivered. He pulled his cloak tight around him.

Faustus pointed at me again. 'You, Mervyn, want to get your hands on Pa's money. And so do you Captain. How will you decide who gets the money?'

'No one's getting my money,' Vortigern wailed.

Faustus looked disgusted. 'Then the Scots and the Saxons will join their forces, kill you and split your money.'

Vortigern said, 'Oh.'

'The only way you can be saved is if you pay one of them to fight the other. Then you only have one enemy. You pay them off with half your money and we all get to live.'

Vortigern's face lit up and glowed like a candle. 'That's brilliant, Faustus. Expensive, but brilliant.'

I leaned forward. 'You could send most of your fortune to one of your forts in the West. To Wales. When the winner claims your gold you will show them your treasure chests are nearly empty.'

'Even more brilliant,' Vortigern chuckled.

'No it's not,' Faustus snapped. 'I was just about to say that myself.' He glared at me. I knew I had made an enemy.

'So who do we make peace with?' Vortigern asked.

The captain spread his hands. 'Well the enemy that gets here first.'

'That's going to be the Saxons,' said the more muddied messenger, who had come from Kent.

And so it was agreed. When the Saxon armies drew near, some poor messenger would go out to meet them and offer to pay them to fight the Scots. A monk from Vortigern's chapel would write a letter.

The messenger from York said, 'I'm not taking a letter to them. They might kill me. They're vicious.'

'I'm not taking it. They might torture me. They're ruthless,' the messenger from Kent added.

'No,' Faustus smiled. 'We want someone worthless. Someone we won't miss if they cut him into a hundred pieces. His eyes gleamed and they turned on me. 'We will send young Mervyn.'

'You can't send me,' I squawked.

'Why not?'

'Because... because... because I don't want to go,' I said and the words fell from my lips as limp as boiled cabbage.

I went.

3

The Villains

The Saxons moved swiftly as hawks and were in the valley below the palace in just three days. I rode a small pony out to meet them. Faustus said the old monk, Benedict, would go with me and so a man in a brown, hooded robe rode silently alongside.

The smell of the Saxon army hit me when I was still a hundred yards from them. It was the smell of horse-flesh, sweat and dried blood. Two men stepped forward and walked out to meet us. One was a little bit larger than an oak tree but smaller than a mountain. The other was no thicker than a twig from that oak tree and I was sure a breeze would blow him away. A lady on a white pony followed and watched from ten yards behind the two men.

'I am Hengist,' the large Saxon said. 'Commander of the Saxons.'

'And I'm Horsa,' the little one with a weasel face squeaked. 'I'm his brother you know. We're going to smash you like worms under a horse's hoof. Squidge, splat, scrunch, flat.'

I was just about to give them the message I had been told to deliver, when the man in the brown robe leaned towards me. 'But who is the beautiful young woman on the white pony?' he asked.

My jaw fell to my chest. I knew that voice and the white beard. It was King Vortigern himself, in disguise. 'What are you doing here? If they know you're the king they'll kill you here and now and Britain will fall.'

'I'm just here to make sure you get the message right,' he mumbled.

'Here to make sure I don't offer them too much of your precious money,' I replied.

'We demand you surrender,' Hengist was saying.

'Yes,' Horsa added. 'And we'll take your king's place.'

I nodded. 'King Vortigern has a better idea,' I said. 'Britain is being ruined by Scots from the north. If you drive them back he will give you the richest county in Britain. He'll give you Kent.'

Hengist and Horsa looked at one another. 'Why should we agree?'

'Because there'll be no fighting and no one gets killed. We live in peace together and share the goodness of the land.'

'And share the gold in the king's treasure house?' little Horsa asked.

'No,' I said sharply, just as I was told.

'Yes,' Vortigern whispered in my ear.

'What?' I gasped.

'Find out who the lovely lady is,' he ordered.

I looked at Hengist and my face must have been like a sheep's. 'Erm... who is the lovely lady?'

He looked over his shoulder. 'That's my daughter Rowena. The most priceless jewel in my life.'

Vortigern was mumbling quickly in my ear and I tried to repeat what he was saying. 'Vortigern says... I mean... King Vortigern will give you the County of Kent AND half of all his treasures... and half of all the taxes he raises each year... every year... if you will give him the lady's land in carriage... sorry... I mean her hand in marriage.'

'What do you say?' Hengist asked his daughter.

'I don't know I'm sure. Last year you wanted to marry me off to that spotty little lord in Gaul.'

'This is a better deal,' Horsa said.

'What's this King Vertical like?' she demanded.

Vortigern threw back his hood and stepped forward. 'A mighty warrior and a handsome king. It is I, sweet Rowena. It is I.'

His old knees creaked as he knelt on the damp grass and spread his arms.

'What do you say, girl?' Hengist asked.

'He's a bit old, isn't he? A bit of a wrinkly. He's older than you. I didn't know there was anyone older than you, Dad.'

Hengist's heavy face turned darker than the rain clouds in the sky above us. 'Just do as you're told, young lady.'

She stuck out her beautiful lips in a pout like a trout and sniffed. 'Do I get to be queen?' she asked.

'Oh yes,' Vortigern said.

She blew out her cheeks. 'Oh all right then.'

And so Britain was lost to the savage Saxons for the sake of a maiden's hand in marriage.

Vortigern was kneeling beside me and muttering something. 'What was that, sire?' I said.

'I said... help me up. My knee has locked and I can't stand up again.'

As I think I said, Vortigern was a fool. He was also an old fool... and they're the worst sort.

4

The Rulers

For a month or so, Vortigern was happy as a donkey in a field of clover. He had a new young wife while Hengist and Horsa kept their promise and drove the Scots out of North Britain.

The brothers returned to Vortigern's palace with sweat on their horses and blood on their swords. And that was wrong. It's a three-day ride from the borders of Scotland to our palace. The blood should have dried days ago.

Hengist pushed his mighty shoulder

against the door to the great hall. Horsa scuttled in behind him. 'Fetch me beef and bread,' Hengist roared at me as he marched up to the great chair at the head of the table – Vortigern's throne really – and sat on it.

'And wine for me,' Horsa said as he sat at his brother's right hand – the queen's place. A handful of Saxon bodyguards clattered in with a rattle of armour.

I said nothing. You don't argue with men who smell of fresh blood.

By the time I returned from the kitchens with wooden boards heavy with food, King Vortigern was entering the room with Queen Rowena.

'Hello, Dad,' the queen said to Hengist. 'I hear you done good up north.'

'We did, girl, but it was hard work. Slaughter every morning, massacres in the afternoon and executions in the evening,' Horsa giggled. Hengist was too busy stuffing bread into his whale-wide mouth.

'Well done, my friends,' Vortigern said. He was smiling under that white beard but his voice was shaking.

Hengist washed down a large piece of beef with his wine and made a disgusting noise. 'Oooops,' he said. 'Well

Vortigern, we've got rid of your Scots and now we can tell you what we're going to do.'

'Go back to Kent and settle down,' Vortigern said, nervous.

'Go back to Kent, yes. We can't live in this dump of a woodworm's paradise. We're planning to take over an old Roman camp. Nice stone buildings. Underfloor heating. Walls round the outside and homes for the troops,' Hengist explained before he threw a beef rib to the floor where his hounds fought over it.

'But we need to give you our orders before we go,' little Horsa said with that sly grin.

'Give me orders?' Vortigern said. 'But I'm the king.'

Hengist, Horsa and Rowena looked at one another and laughed softly. 'King in name, maybe,' Horsa said. 'But we all know we have the real power. The power of the sword.' He patted the hilt of his own weapon.

'So this is what we'll do,' Hengist went on. 'We'll go back to Kent. You will collect the taxes – we're not very good at that sort of thing. And you've been doing it for years.'

'Yes, I'm good at collecting taxes,' the old king nodded.

'And you will pay those taxes to us,' Horsa said.

'What? All of them?'

'I think we may let you keep a tenth,' Hengist said and spread his fat hands as if he were giving Vortigern the greatest gift of jewels.

'But... what do I get?' Vortigern asked.

Horsa grinned his weasel grin. 'You get to keep your life.'

The old man's face grew dark with anger. 'My lords will never allow it. I mean... you've done a good job getting rid of the Scots, but you can't take over the country. My lords will crush you.'

Hengist threw back his head and laughed. He almost choked on some of the great gouts of food in his mouth. He coughed long and hard and at last was able to speak again. 'Tell him, Horsa.'

Horsa shrugged. 'You don't have no lords, my old pal Vortigern. We invited them all to a feast last night. We told them to leave their weapons at the door. We fed them well, then our Saxon knights drew their swords and we killed them all.'

'All?'

'Every last one. As I say, we only let you live because you're useful to us,' Horsa said.

'And because you're married to our dear Rowena,' Hengist put in. 'You wouldn't want us to slay your husband, would you, Weenie-wena?'

'Wouldn't bother me, Pa. You do what you have to do to conquer Britain for us Saxons.'

'Well, not just us Saxons,' Horsa put in. 'We'll dish out land to our friends the Jutes from Jutland and the Angles can look after the north for us – make sure the Scots don't come back.'

'Ah, yes, the Angles,' Hengist said with a rumbling laugh. 'They're already settling their families. They're even calling the place Angle-land.'

'I thought it was England,' Rowena said. 'That's what I heard.'

Her uncle Horsa shrugged. 'Angle-land... England... same thing. Britain is finished. Angles and Saxons rule. End of story.'

King Vortigern looked sicker than a snake that's swallowed a hedgehog. He looked at me, helpless. And later that night we started to make our plans.

Plans to escape.

5

The Wise Man

The Saxons found our treasure chests and emptied them. 'We'll be back for more as soon as you've collected your taxes this year,' they promised before they rode off. The king called me to his chamber. 'The ancient Britons moved west to Wales when the Romans had invaded.'

'I know, sire. I came from Wales to serve you.'

'That's why I need your help,' he said. 'I have lands over there. If I move to Wales I will be safe from these brutal

Saxons and their friends. Will you guide me?'

I liked the idea of going home to the mountains, to the forests full of wild boar and deer for hunting and to the friendly people. 'I will,' I said. 'But will Queen Rowena be happy there?'

'Ahh,' he said. 'I think it better if we don't tell her. She would only betray us to her father.'

'I think it better too, sire,' I nodded. 'I can have a few loyal servants ready to

leave tomorrow evening after it gets dark. By morning light we'll be fifty miles away.'

And so we fled from the place they called England. And a week later we came to my homeland of Wales.

I took Vortigern to Tegwyn, the leader of the Dubonni tribe. Tegwyn welcomed the old king as his master and the tribe began to plan a new home and a new life for Vortigern.

Of course, I had become the king's closest adviser and top servant. I had saved him and he treated me like one of his lords. Of course his other lords had ended up dead. If I had known that I was building a path to my own grave I'd have run back to England.

I knew Vortigern was a fool. I didn't believe Tegwyn could be just as stupid.

The trouble (for me) began when they started to build a new palace at

Dinas Emrys. The men and women of the Dubonni tribe laboured hard all day to build a fine tower of hard, grey mountain stone. But that night when the work stopped...

Vortigern sat up in bed. 'What was that sound like thunder?' he cried.

I was sleeping at his door as his guard. 'Is it the Saxon hordes come to hunt me down? Save me, Mervyn,' he wailed and shivered under his sheepskin bed cover.

Moments later, Tegwyn was at the door. 'Oh, King Vortigern,' he sighed. 'It's your tower. It has fallen down.'

'Oh, is that all?' the king laughed.

Tegwyn promised they would build it up again. And so they did, the next day. But at night when the work stopped... the tower collapsed again.

Every night for a week the Dubonni built the tower and ever night it fell down.

After a week Vortigern asked Tegwyn to get help from a wise man. I was serving wild boar stew when the two men met.

'No need,' Tegwyn said. 'I am famous for being a wise man. Famous, see?'

'So what is the problem, wise Tegwyn,' the king asked.

'It's like this you see. There is an old belief in this part of Britain that says a new house must have a blood sacrifice,' Tegwyn said. Wisely.

'I've heard of that,' Vortigern nodded... almost as wisely.

'Sometimes a human victim is walled up alive,' silly, wise Tegwyn went on.

'Sounds daft to me,' I muttered.

'Sometimes they are killed and their blood mixed with the cement,' the Dubonni chief continued.

'Messy.' I muttered.

'And sometimes the blood of a victim must be sprinkled on the ground,' he added.

I wouldn't want to paddle through that in my bare feet. Or even in my boots. I was disgusted.

Vortigern said, 'So let's kill one of the workmen.'

'No, no! The blood must be the blood of an innocent, fatherless boy.'

Vortigern shook his head. 'I don't know any fatherless boys.' He looked up. 'Except Mervyn here... and he's my best servant. I can't afford to lose him.'

Tegwyn's eyes went narrow. 'Winter will be here soon. You can't afford to delay the building any longer,' he said. He marched to the door and called to his tribesmen. 'Right, lads, give Mervyn here the chop.'

6

The Dragons

I pushed past Tegwyn to the door. 'No, wait. Don't kill me. Killing me will not stop your castle falling down,' I cried. But the swords were drawn. Grim-faced men and women walked steadily towards me. I turned and ran.

I ran outside and through the village, then I took the path that led down the mountain. I knew I was finished. No matter how fast or far I ran they would catch me in the end. My only hope was to hide for a while. When the hunters went past me I could creep back up the hill and beg Vortigern to listen to me.

I threw myself off the track just before the mob came around the corner. There was a crack in the rock. I squeezed myself in as far as I could go. I pushed harder and, suddenly, I fell. It wasn't a crack in the rock. It was the opening to a cave.

The late evening sun lit the inside and shone on a calm lake of black water. Dust and small stones drifted down from the high roof. And I knew. This was a cave beneath the tower. This was the reason the building fell down.

Of course these fools wouldn't believe something as simple as that could wreck their fine palace plans. So by the time I had slipped out of the narrow entrance I had a new legend ready for the simple minds of the simple king and the simpler people.

I ran back up the hill. Tegwyn was standing at the top of the path and drew his sword. He blew a hunting horn to bring the hunters back and gather the rest of the tribe. Vortigern came to the door.

'So good of you to come back,' the king said. 'You saved my life so I will repay you.'

'Thank you, sire,' I said.

'I will make sure your death is quick and clean. None of that being walled up alive to die slowly. Bend your neck forward and Tegwyn will take it off with a single stroke. I'll catch the blood in this bowl.'

No,' I groaned. 'I know the real reason the tower is falling down. I found a cave beneath the tower floor.'

'That wouldn't make the tower fall,' Tegwyn said. He ran his thumb along the edge of his sword to test to see if it was sharp enough.

'No. Listen. Beneath this ground there is

a pool. And in the pool there are two dragons – a red dragon and a white dragon. Every night they fight and it's their struggle that brings the tower down.'

The villagers gasped in wonder. Vortigern's watery, hazel eyes marvelled. 'Amazing. What a clever boy you are. Here, lads, maybe we should give the stupid, wise chief the chop instead.'

Tegwyn saw the crowd turn towards him. He turned. He ran. No one followed. They all wanted to hear what I had to say.

'Now, young Mervyn, what can we do about it?'

'The red dragon is Wales, the white dragon is Saxon England. When the red dragon defeats the white then peace will return,' I said.

Vortigern cried, 'So, all we have to do is defeat the Saxons. Right, lads. Of to fight the Saxons...'

A day later they were ready to march back east to England and war. I didn't care. I said I'd stay behind and build a new palace – on a safer ground – for Vortigern when he returned with the heads of Hengist and Horsa. 'And Rowena,' the old king added bitterly.

Of course Vortigern never did get to defeat the Saxons. That was down to another British leader – the man they knew as Arthur. He was a simple-minded son of a warrior chief. He had a bit of luck and won a few battles... with me making the plans for him.

By then my name – Mervyn – had been changed to the English 'Merlin'.

With my sharp wit and Arthur's strong arm we went to battle together.

One day I will write of Arthur's adventures and he will be a British hero and a legend for all times. Oh, not because he's a great hero... but because I am a great teller of tales.

I think I will start with a sword that is stuck fast in a stone. Only the true king of Britain can pull it out. It's nonsense, of course, but people believe most things if they are impossible enough.

So, let's see... Arthur, a sword in a stone and a round table for his band of knights.

Do you think people will believe that two thousand years from now?

Of course they will.

The True Story

The Romans left Britain around 410 AD. They left the British people with no defence. The Picts and Scots attacked from the north and the Angles, Saxons and Jutes from across the North Sea.

The history writers of those days said Vortigern was King of The British and came up with the plan of using Hengist and Horsa to drive the Picts out. The king fell in love with Rowena and gave the Saxons more than they deserved. The problem was the Saxon brothers decided to stay. They killed the British lords at a feast and made Vortigern rule for them.

Vortigern went off to Wales where his new palace kept falling down each night after it was built. The legend says Merlin was picked to be a sacrifice. He told a story of the two dragons fighting in a pool below the building and saved himself. The legend goes on the say that Merlin went on to be King Arthur's closest friend in his battle against the Saxon invaders.

The tales of Merlin and Arthur are mostly legend, though the British really did defeat the Saxons in battles at that time. And when Dinas Emrys was excavated in the 1950s they really did find a deep pool beneath it. The red dragon became the symbol of the Welsh.

Some writers think Vortigern was a legend and never existed. We may never know.

YOU TRY...

1. Imagine a Saxon Army is marching towards your town. They will make you their slave. You have to flee with just a pony to carry things. What FIVE things would you take with you? Why would you choose each one? What would you miss most?

2. King Vortigern is rich and very proud. He would probably have a minstrel to sing him songs each night as he feasted by the fireside. Of course the minstrels would sing about the great things Vortigern had done and the battles he had won, how the people of Britain loved him. The minstrel would sing of the great things Vortigern would do in future. Can YOU write a rhyming minstrel song that would make the king want to give you food, a cosy bed for the night and even a purse of gold? Write any poem you like, but it might begin...

'Oh Vortigern, our mighty king,

Of your great deeds I want to sing.

3. There are no pictures of the cruel and vicious brothers Hengist and Horsa. (The pictures in the story are how the artist thinks he *might* have looked.) How do YOU think the warriors and their sister may have looked? Draw your own pictures to show this ruthless family.

Terry Deary's Saxon Tales

The Witch who Faced the Fire

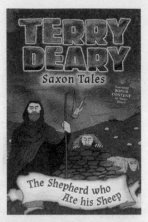

The Shepherd who Ate his Sheep

The Lord who Lost his Head

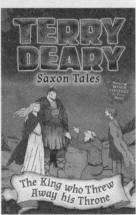

The King who Threw Away his Throne

If you liked this book why not look out
for the rest of Terry Deary's Saxon Tales?

Terry Deary's Shakespeare Tales

Meet Shakespeare and his theatre
company in Terry Deary's
Shakespeare Tales.

Look out for more Terry Deary Tales

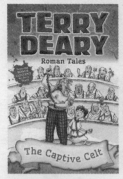

Egyptian Tales   Tudor Tales
Greek Tales   Victorian Tales
Knights' Tales   Viking Tales
Pirate Tales   World War I Tales
Roman Tales   World War II Tales

Visit www.bloomsbury.com
for more information